S0-AYP-638

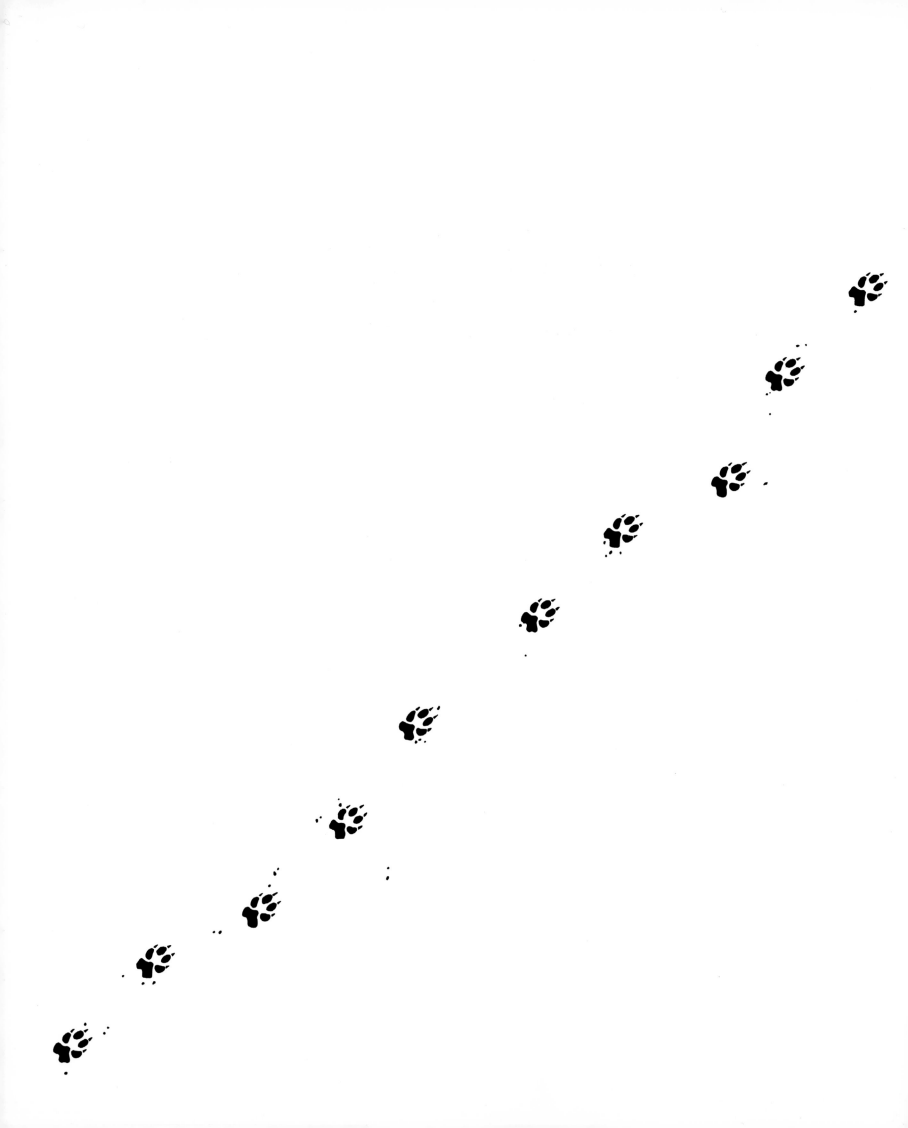

WHITE FANG

Adapted from the novel by Jack London

Text by Arsene Lutin
Illustrations by Antoine Guilloppe

Deep within a snow-covered forest, two wolves hunt.
Kiche is half-wolf, half-dog and has a deep red coat.
Her partner, One Eye, is a big gray wolf.
They are a handsome pair—strong and mighty.
And they love each other.
Everything they do is in unison, like mirror images of one another.
And, today, they catch a large moose!
Eat or be eaten, this is the Law of Nature in this frozen land.

But the snow soon begins to melt, and the following spring Kiche gives birth
to a wolf cub in a small moss-covered cave.
Nature flourishes with new life, too: bright green leaves sprout on tree branches,
colorful flowers bloom in fields, and once again, streams flow through valleys and hills.
But everything is not always perfect. Kiche must care for her cub and keep him safe
from the predators that lurk in the shadows.

One day, while his Kiche was out hunting, the cub went exploring
outside of his cave for the first time.
The young cub is on an adventure discovering the world!
The flowers, grass, and smooth stones in the stream astonish and amaze him.
He meets field mice, squirrels, and rabbits.
The cub playfully scampers around trying to catch them but,
more often than not, ends up flat on his back or flat on his face!

During one of his escapades, the cub finds himself muzzle
to muzzle with a dangerous lynx.
Kiche bears her teeth and tries to protect her baby.
But the lynx will not back down.
Suddenly, the crack of a gunshot echoes through the air—
it's Kiche's friend, Gray Beaver.
The lynx runs off, but the cub is frightened.
He snarls at Gray Beaver.
His teeth are as white as snow.
"You will be called White Fang," Gray Beaver tells him.

Gray Beaver, a tough but fair man, takes White Fang and Kiche back to his camp.
The young cub is torn between his instinct to obey and his instinct for freedom.
But he soon accepts this man's home and is amazed by his talents for making
canvas caves and blazing fires.
White Fang respects and obeys these men.

However, his relationship with the other dogs in the camp is a different story.
They all sense that White Fang is not only a dog but also a wolf!
They snarl when he approaches, but White Fang never gives in—he is a survivor!
And he obeys his master, Gray Beaver.

But Gray Beaver soon decides to part with Kiche and finds her a home with another man.
White Fang watches his mother sail away and tries to join her,
but Gray Beaver commands him to stay.
The wolf cub whimpers sadly as Kiche disappears into the distance.
He feels alone in the world.

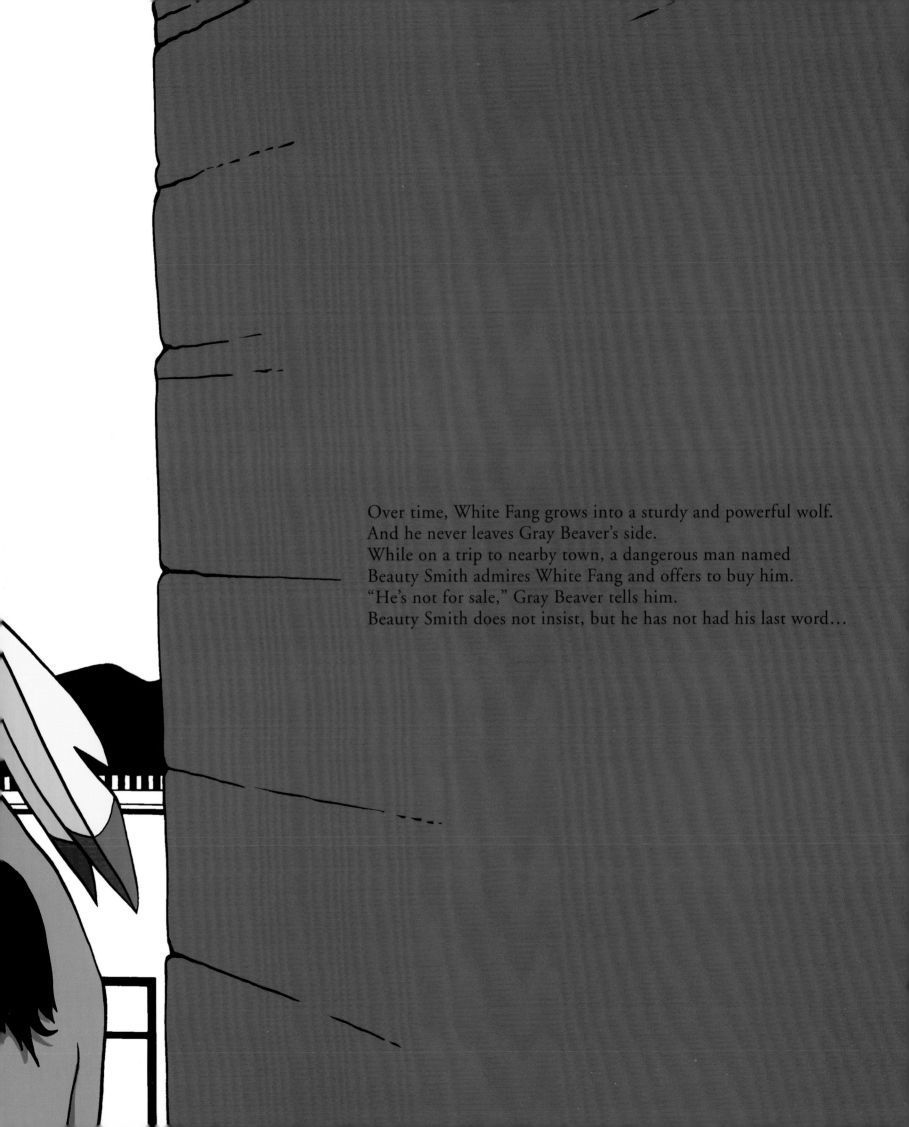

Over time, White Fang grows into a sturdy and powerful wolf.
And he never leaves Gray Beaver's side.
While on a trip to nearby town, a dangerous man named
Beauty Smith admires White Fang and offers to buy him.
"He's not for sale," Gray Beaver tells him.
Beauty Smith does not insist, but he has not had his last word…

In fact, Beauty Smith will not stop at anything until he owns White Fang.
He is a cowardly and deceitful man, and he tricks Gray Beaver into selling White Fang to him.
And then he turns White Fang into fighting dog in hopes that he will make him lots of money.

White Fang's wolf instincts make him an undefeated fighter.
Now, the only law is to win or to be defeated.
And White Fang must fight to stay alive.
He lives this life of hardship and torment for a long time until one day
a mine engineer, named Weedon Scott, enters the barn where White Fang
is wrestling with another dog.
As soon as Weedon Scott sets his eyes upon White Fang he knows that
they are one in the same… they both have a broken and gentle nature
beneath a fierce and wild appearance.
He is determined to rescue White Fang from the cruel clutches of Beauty Smith.
So he convinces Beauty Smith to sell White Fang to him.
But it may be too late for White Fang—he was badly injured in his last battle
with another dog.

Weedon Scott takes care of White Fang and tends to his injuries.
He wants to teach him a life without hatred, and life full of kindness.
But White Fang is wary.
He has been betrayed so many times in the past and it's hard for him to trust this man.
So Weedon Scott is patient and gentle and gives White Fang freedom.
Day after day, he slowly offers the wolf fresh meat.
And eventually, he lays his hand on White Fang's large head and starts stroking him…

Little by little, White Fang realizes that the hand of man is capable of gentle strokes, kindness, and affection.
The strong wolf begins to feel very attached to his new master.
And a new feeling overcomes him.
It is stronger and greater than the respect he had for Gray Beaver and the fear he had for Beauty Smith.
It is love.
When it is time for Weedon Scott to return to his home, White Fang is by his side!
The two make the homeward-bound journey together.

White Fang thrives in his new home where the days are sunny and warm!
And he lives a peaceful life with Weedon Scott's family.
They are affectionate, gentle, and giving towards White Fang.
Even Collie, the family dog, eventually learns to play with the mighty wolf
and they soon come to love each other, too!

One evening, while White Fang is asleep in front of his master's bedroom, he is woken by a sound coming from the floor below.
Alert and attentive, White Fang slinks downstairs to find a criminal has broken into the house!
White Fang, a loyal protector to his family, springs at the intruder!
During the fight, White Fang is wounded by this man and is in danger of losing his life.

However, Weedon Scott rescues White Fang and he is saved!
He is a hero among the family.
Everyone carefully nurtures their protective friend until his wounds heal
and he is strong and healthy again.
When White Fang has made a full recovery, it is time for him to return home
to the family's house.
He arrives and is surprised to see Collie surrounded by a magnificent litter of puppies—
White Fang is a dad!
The puppies, eager to have some fun with their father, scamper up to the wolf
as he patiently lies down on his side so they can climb upon him and play.
From this day forward, White Fang lives a happy life with Collie and his children by his side.
The rumbling wolf lying deep within White Fang can now rest in peace,
thanks to that very special feeling… love.

General Manager: Gauthier Auzou
Senior Editor: Aude Sarrazin
English Version Editor: Rebecca Frazer
Translation from French: Susan Allen-Maurin
Graphics and layout (English Version): Annaïs Tassone
Production: Amélie Moncarré
Original title: CROC-BLANC
© Auzou Publishing, Paris (France), 2013 (English version)

ISBN: 978-2-27338-2145-9

Printed in China, December 2012